THE TECHNOLOGY TAIL

For Bobbie Lowe -
Queen of Digital Footprint Education!
~ Love Julia

BOYS TOWN Press
Boys Town, Nebraska

Written by **JULIA COOK**

Illustrated by **ANITA DuFALLA**

The Technology Tail
Text and Illustrations Copyright © 2017 by Father Flanagan's Boys' Home
ISBN 978-1-944882-13-6

Published by the Boys Town Press
14100 Crawford St.
Boys Town, NE 68010

For a Boys Town Press catalog, call **1-800-282-6657**
or visit our website: **BoysTownPress.org**

Publisher's Cataloging-in-Publication Data

Names: Cook, Julia, 1964- author. | DuFalla, Anita, illustrator.

Title: The technology tail : a digital footprint story / written by Julia Cook ; illustrated by Anita DuFalla.

Description: Boys Town, NE : Boys Town Press, [2017] | Series: Communicate with confidence ; no. 4. | Audience: Children, grades 1-6. | Summary: "The Technology Tail" uses rhymes and colorful illustrations to offer a timeless message to a new generation learning to navigate the fast-changing digital age. Whether sending a photo or making a comment, "Screen" wants kids to know their posts -- the kind and the cruel -- will follow them for a very long time and will influence their friendships.–Publisher.

Identifiers: ISBN: 978-1-944882-13-6

Subjects: LCSH: Online social networks--Juvenile fiction. | Online etiquette--Juvenile fiction. | Internet-- Social aspects--Juvenile fiction. | Social media--Juvenile fiction. | Bullying--Prevention-- Juvenile fiction. | Cyberbullying--Prevention--Juvenile fiction. | Internet and children-- Juvenile fiction. | Interpersonal relations in children--Juvenile fiction. | Children-- Life skills guides. | CYAC: Online social networks--Fiction. | Online etiquette--Fiction. | Social media-- Fiction. | Internet--Social aspects--Fiction. | Bullying--Prevention--Fiction. | Cyberbullying-- Prevention--Fiction. | Interpersonal relations--Fiction. | Behavior--Fiction. | Etiquette-- Fiction. | Conduct of life. | BISAC: JUVENILE FICTION / Social Themes / Manners & Etiquette. | JUVENILE FICTION / Social Themes / Friendship. | JUVENILE FICTION / Social Themes / Bullying. | EDUCATION / Counseling / General.

Classification: LCC: PZ7.C76984 T43 2017 | DDC: [E]--dc23

Printed in the United States
10 9 8 7 6 5 4 3 2

Boys Town Press is the publishing division of Boys Town,
a national organization serving children and families.

"I do! I talk all the time.
And I have a lot to say.
If you hit send or post those words,
You will ruin your entire day...

and your
entire
tomorrow
too!"

"Huh? Why?"

4

"Because it will hurt your tail."

"My what?"

"Your TECHNOLOGY TAIL."

"I DON'T have a tail!"

"Yes, you do. Everyone does.
It follows you day and night.
Everything you pass to others through me,
Is attached to you for life!

Everything you post sticks to your tail,
And becomes a part of you.
Once you hit send, it's on there for good,
And there's nothing you can do...

SERIOUSLY,
I thought you knew!"

"**Nope.** Didn't know that."

"*Just look at your tail. See all these things...*
These are gifts you have given yourself.
Your tail gets a gift when you post something nice,
Or when you use your words to help."

"But when you post things that are hurtful or mean,
Your tail gets a bruise, scratch or tear.
Then others feel bad because of you,
And the mean things you've chosen to share.

And since I'm stuck in the middle of it all, I turn into an

IRRESPONSIBLE
MEAN
SCREEN...

and I worry about that a lot!"

8

"What really stinks about my job is that, over time, people start to develop

'keyboard courage.'"

"What's that?"

"It means they post things online that they would never say or do to a person face-to-face. And some of that stuff can be really mean and inappropriate!"

"Did you know that every time you post a put-down, the person who gets it needs 10 pull-ups just to feel better! That's **10 sincere compliments...** for just **one put-down!** That's a lot!!!"

"I am your screen... *I SEE it all.*
Everything you send goes through me.
See, here's that picture you posted last week,
When you and your friends climbed that tree."

"Now THAT was a BLAST!"

"This one's neat. It's a wonderful gift!
It's that picture you took of a stray.
You did all you could to find that kitty a home,
Now that was a REALLY GREAT DAY!"

"Here are the selfies you took with your friends,
On the day when you went to the mall.
I can't believe how happy you look.
And that friend of yours is **SO TALL!**"

"Yeah, that was
awesome!
Hey! How come I didn't get a
gift for that one?"

"Well, you left out one friend on purpose,
Then posted pictures to put her down.
My friend watched her face
   when she saw them online,
And her smile turned into a frown."

"**Oh yeah,** she told her mom about it,
and her mom called my mom and I got
grounded for **TWO WHOLE DAAAYS.**"

"If you were my kid, I would have grounded you for

TWO YEARS!"

"Well then it's a good
thing screens don't
have kids."

14

"Hey! This wasn't a mean post. How come I got a scratch for it?"

"Because it made the person you sent it to feel bad."

"Well then she read it wrong. Some people are SO sensitive!"

I can only do so much!!

"Yeah, that happens a lot.

Unfortunately, I can only post words and a few symbols, not the human expressions and hidden meanings that go along with them.

Talking online is easy, but it will **NEVER** be as powerful as face-to-face communication. Hopefully, you humans will start to realize that."

15

"What's this?"

"That's a hole."

"How'd I get that?"

"Holes come from posts
that are not very smart.
Like when you shared test
answers in language arts."

"You know about
that, too?"

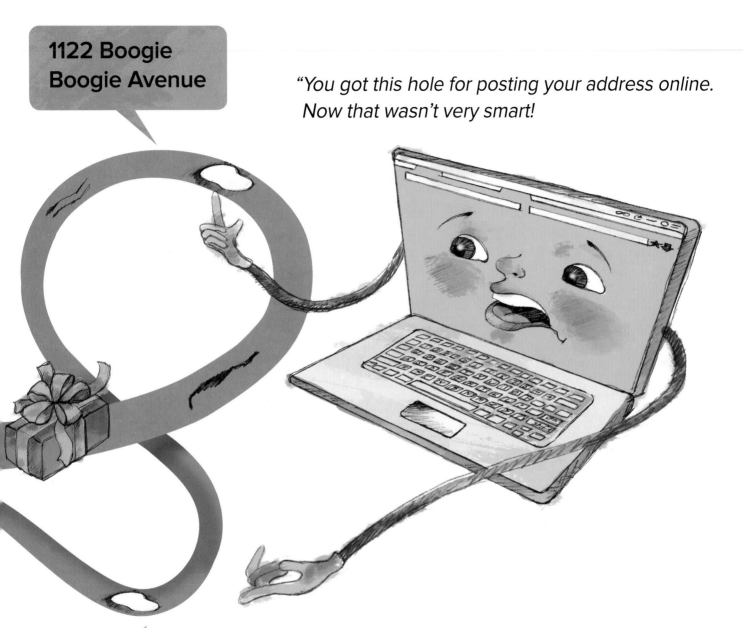

17

"What about this one?"

"Oh, that happened when you shared your password with your friends.

Now why would you go and do that???

Your password is private information between **me** **and** **you**...
not you and the whole wide world!!!

How can I possibly protect you when that happens?"

"There's no way you know about all of that stuff!"

18

"Oh yes... and it's not just me that knows.
The people who know where to look,
Can find everything you've ever sent.
It's like all you have done in a book!"

"You have to really think about what you're doing,
When you're posting online.
Because that technology tail of yours,
Will follow you through time.

You'll end up dragging it around,
Every single day.
And believe you me, a wounded tail...
Will surely get in your way."

"How?"

"A TECHNOLOGY TAIL *that is bruised, scratched or torn,*
Tells others that you are unkind.
They won't want to hang out with you,
Because they're afraid of what they might find."

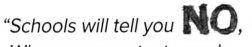

"Schools will tell you **NO**,
Whenever you try to apply.
All the scratches, bruises and tears on your tail,
Will show them you've made others cry."

We only hire
GIFTED
TECHNOLOGY
TAILS

"When employers see holes and wounds,
They won't want to hire you.
They will assume you're irresponsible online,
And that you say stuff that's mean and untrue."

23

"But look... right now your technology tail's pretty good!
You've posted so many great things!
If you keep it up, you'll be surprised...
By the gifts a great tail can bring!"

Move over tail
Here
I come!

“Like what?”

“Like a good right now and an
even better later... and a much
happier SCREEN...

What’s posted today will matter tomorrow.
It just isn’t all about now.
You have to think past the end of your nose,
And I can show you how.”

"Put on a pair of **'Think Gloves'**
Before you touch the keys.
They'll filter out the stuff that's not good.
They look a lot like these..."

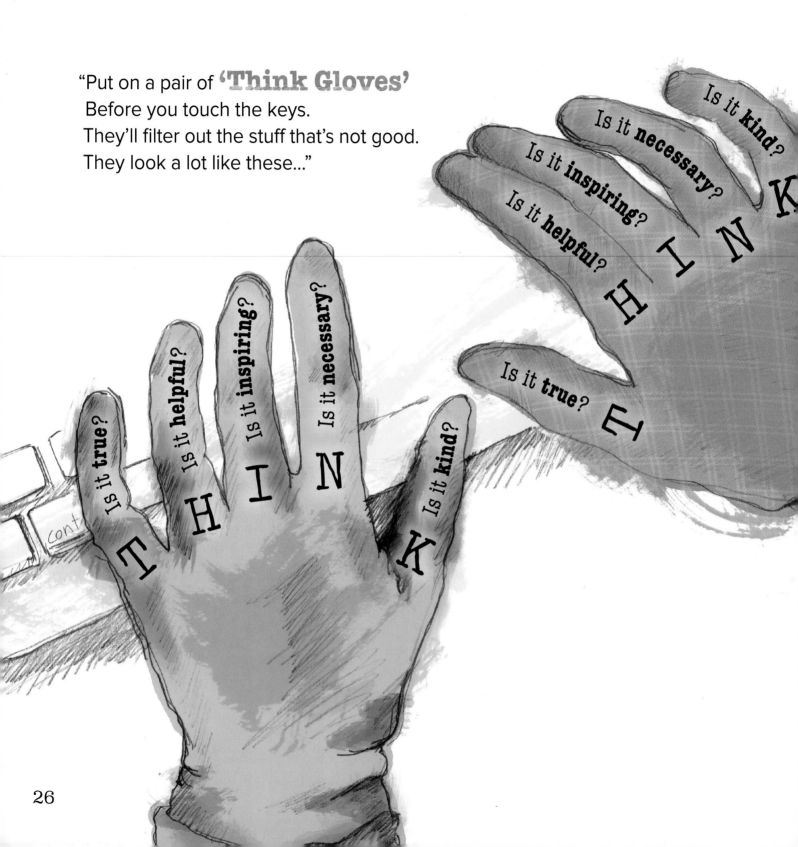

"How do they work?"

"Ask yourself these five questions...

THINK BEFORE YOU POST

T – Is it **TRUE**?

H – Is it **HELPFUL**?

I – Is it **INSPIRING**?

N – Is it **NECESSARY**?

K – Is it **KIND**?

And if you can honestly answer **YES**, then
Post,
Forward,
Text,
Send and
Tweet away.

You won't even have to guess."

THINK
before you post

THINK
before you send

27

"But if the answer to any of those questions...
Ends up being 'NO,'
Let the **'Think Gloves'** stop your post.
Hit DELETE, it's the best way to go."

DELETE

28

"Always remember,
YOU are in charge.
You choose what goes on your tail.
If you filter your words correctly,
*Your actions will **NEVER** fail.*"

"Then I won't have to worry about being the **IRRESPONSIBLE MEAN SCREEN** *EVER AGAIN...*

which will make my life
and yours a **WHOLE LOT BETTER!**"

WHAT'S ON YOUR TAIL?

TECHNOLOGY IS AWESOME... but children sometimes need lots of help managing and using it wisely so it enriches, rather than wrecks, their lives. Here are a few tips to help you guide children toward creating a healthy digital footprint:

1. **Go online with your children** and help them navigate social media and other websites. Use this time to explain your expectations and how to respect technology.

2. **Monitor online access** by placing the family computer in a central location and limiting the use of smartphones, tablets and laptops to public spaces in the home. Set boundaries, including time limits, limits on the type of content they can access, and when and where they can use their digital devices.

3. **Unplug and recharge ALL digital devices** during family routines, such as mealtime and bedtime. If a child uses his or her smartphone as an alarm, replace it with an inexpensive alarm clock.

4. **Tell and continually remind children** never to post personal information (home address, passwords, account numbers, phone numbers, etc.) on social networking sites.

5. **Explain, remind and reinforce this safety rule**: Never meet face-to-face with someone you only know from the internet, and if someone asks to meet you, tell a parent, older sibling, teacher or trusted adult.

BOYS TOWN.
Parenting

For more parenting information,
visit boystown.org/parenting.

31

Boys Town Press Books by Julia Cook
Kid-friendly books to teach social skills

COMMUNICATE with Confidence

A book series to help kids master the art of communicating.

Well, I Can Top That! — Written by Julia Cook, Illustrated by Anita DuFalla — 978-1-934490-57-0

Gas Happens! What to Do When It Happens to You — Written by Julia Cook, Illustrated by Anita DuFalla — 978-1-934490-76-1

Decibella and her 6-inch Voice — Written by Julia Cook, Illustrated by Anita DuFalla — 978-1-934490-58-7

The Technology Tail — A Digital Footprint Story — Written by Julia Cook, Illustrated by Anita DuFalla — 978-1-944882-13-6

Making Friends Is an Art! — 978-1-934490-30-3

Tease Monster — 978-1-934490-47-1

Peer Pressure Gauge — 978-1-934490-48-8

I Want to Be the Only Dog — Written by Julia Cook — 978-1-934490-86-0

Table Talk — A book about table manners — 978-1-934490-97-6

The Judgmental Flower — Written by Julia Cook, Illustrated by Anita DuFalla — 978-1-944882-05-1

Building RELATIONSHIPS

A book series to help kids get along.

Other Titles:
Cliques Just Don't Make Cents *and* Hygiene You Stink!

BEST ME I Can Be!

To reinforce the social skills RJ learns in each book, accompanying poster sets and activity guides are available.

I Just Want to Do It My Way! — 978-1-934490-43-3

Thanks for the Feedback — 978-1-934490-49-5

I Can't Believe You Said That! — 978-1-934490-67-9

Other Titles: The Worst Day of My Life Ever!, I Just Don't Like the Sound of NO!, Sorry, I Forgot to Ask!, and Teamwork Isn't My Thing, and I Don't Like to Share!

A book series to help kids take responsibility for their behavior.

Responsible ME!

That Rule Doesn't Apply to Me! — Written by Julia Cook, Illustrated by Anita DuFalla — 978-1-934490-98-3

The Procrastinator — 978-1-944882-09-9

Other Title: Baditude!, But It's not My Fault *and* Cheaters Never Prosper

A story about autism understanding and acceptance.

Uniquely Wired! — A Story about Autism and Its Gifts — Written by Julia Cook, Illustrated by Anita DuFalla — 978-1-944882-19-8

BOYS TOWN® Press

BoysTownPress.org

For information on Boys Town, its Education Model®, Common Sense Parenting®, and training programs:
boystowntraining.org | boystown.org/parenting
training@BoysTown.org | 1-800-545-5771

For parenting and educational books and other resources:
BoysTownPress.org
btpress@BoysTown.org | 1-800-282-6657